Henry and Pawl
and the Round Yellow Ball

written and illustrated by Tom Casmer and Mary GrandPré

DIAL BOOKS FOR YOUNG READERS   NEW YORK

Published by Dial Books for Young Readers
A division of Penguin Young Readers Group ✳ 345 Hudson
Street, New York, New York, 10014 ✳ Copyright © 2005 by Mary
GrandPré and Tom Casmer ✳ All rights reserved ✳ Designed by Kimi
Weart and Jasmin Rubero ✳ Text set in New Century Schoolbook
Manufactured in China on acid-free paper ✳ Library of Congress Cataloging-in-
Publication Data ✳ GrandPré, Mary. ✳ Henry and Pawl and the round yellow ball /
written and illustrated by Tom Casmer and Mary GrandPré. ✳ p.   cm. ✳ Summary: After
Henry receives the art kit he wanted for his birthday, his dog's toy ball leads him to create the
special painting he hoped he could make. ✳ ISBN 0-8037-2784-4 ✳ [1. Painting—Fiction.
2. Dogs—Fiction. 3. Balls (Sporting goods)—Fiction. 4. Birthdays—Fiction.] ✳ I. Casmer, Tom.
II. Title. PZ7.G76612He 2005 [E]—dc21 ✳ 2003002355

The art was created using pencil, watercolor, acrylics,
and pastels on watercolor paper.

For little artists with big dreams
—M.G.P.

For Ian, Megan, and Cooper. Finally . . .
—T.C.

Ever since Henry was a baby, he loved
his dog Pawl and making pictures.
Ever since Pawl was a puppy, he loved
Henry and his round yellow ball.

The day before Henry's birthday, he saw just what he wanted in Mr. Cooper's art store...

The Mighty Masters Art Kit.

"With a kit like that, I could make the best picture ever," Henry told Pawl. "Something important, something special, something really great!"

Pawl saw something in the window too. *Mmmm...my ball. It's really great,* thought Pawl.

That night Henry dreamed of the art kit and the
wonderful things he could create.

The next morning Henry flew out of bed.
"Today is my birthday!" he shouted.

When it was time for the birthday cake, Henry made a wish.
"Oh, Pawl," Henry whispered, "I wished with all my might."
Then Henry's mom and dad brought in a huge present.

Henry and his dad put the art kit together in his bedroom.
Pawl helped too.

"It's super," said Henry.

So super, thought Pawl, nudging his ball up onto the stool.

"And now," said Henry, "for something . . . important, something special, something . . . GREAT!"

But nothing looked quite right.

"I don't get it. These pictures are okay, but they're not important, or special, or great."

Henry swatted at the crumpled balls of paper.

Pawl swatted his ball onto Henry's lap.

That night, Henry had the worst dream ever.

And in the morning Henry called out:
"C'mon Pawl, there's gotta be something out here
to draw . . . something bigger . . . something better . . .
something super-duper!"

My ball. So yellow. So round. So super-duper! thought Pawl.

"Hmmm . . . flowers are pretty, but everybody paints those," said Henry.

He tossed the ball.

My ball. So yellow. So round. Bounces so high! thought Pawl.

"That's a big statue, but kinda boring," said Henry.

He threw the ball again and this time it bounced into . . .

Mrs. Gibber's candy store.

"Oh my goodness! Not in the gumdrops!" shrieked Mrs. Gibber
as she picked up the ball and tossed it away.

"Oops! So sorry, Mrs. G.," said Henry.

Pawl ran after his ball. Henry ran after Pawl.

They looked everywhere.

But the ball was lost.
"I'm sorry Pawl. C'mon, we'd better get home."

Now all Henry wanted was to help Pawl feel better.

"How about a nice treat?" he asked. But Pawl just turned away.

It's not yellow. It's not round. And it's not my ball, thought Pawl.

"You really miss that old ball, don't you buddy?" said Henry.

"I wish . . . hey . . . wait!"

Henry sat down at the easel. He picked up a brush.

Paint spattered. Scissors chattered. Glitter gobbed.

Henry made picture after picture. When he was done, Henry called out, "Hey, Mom, Dad, I have a plan. Will you help me?"

Henry and his mom and dad hung his pictures all
over town. Pawl helped too.

Now all they could do was wait . . .

and wait.

The next day there was a knock at the door.
"Henry!" his mom called.
"There's someone here to see
you and Pawl."

A man stood at the doorway. "I believe this belongs to you," he told Pawl.

"So yellow. So round. So good. My ball!" Pawl barked.

"Gee, mister," said Henry, "we forgot to offer a reward."

"Oh, that's quite all right," said the man. "If you don't mind, I'll just keep this great picture."

"MY picture?" Henry smiled. "Thanks, mister!"

After that, Henry found wonderful things to paint . . .

everywhere. And Pawl . . . was always happy to help!